The Most Thankful Thing

by Lisa McCourt
Illustrated by Cyd Moore

SCHOLASTIC INC.
New York Toronto London Auckland Sydney
Mexico City New Delhi Hong Kong Buenos Aires

For my Greg, Tuck, and Lily Kate,
with all the thankfulness in the world.
— L.M.

For Rob, with love and gratitude.
— C.M.

Text copyright © 2004 by Lisa McCourt.
Illustrations copyright © 2004 by Cyd Moore.
All rights reserved. Published by Scholastic Inc.
SCHOLASTIC, CARTWHEEL BOOKS, and associated logos
are trademarks and/or registered trademarks of Scholastic Inc.

Library of Congress Cataloging-in-Publication Data available

ISBN 0-439-65083-6

10 9 8 7 6 5 4 3 2 1   04 05 06 07 08

Printed in Singapore 46 • First Scholastic printing, October 2004

One morning, I found Mama sitting real still, all by herself. Mama never did that.

"Whatcha doing?" I asked her.

Mama smiled. "I'm giving thanks," she said. "I'm thinking about my whole life and remembering all the wonderful things I have to be thankful for."

I asked Mama, "In your whole long, long, long life, what are you the very most thankful for?"

"Oh, that's an easy one," said Mama. "But you have to guess what it is."

I ran to get Mama's big scrapbook. I knew all her most favorite memories were in there.

"Wow, summer camp looks like so much fun," I said. "Was that your most thankful thing?"

"Summer camp was great. We toasted marshmallows and sang songs and slept in sleeping bags and looked for animal footprints."

pocahontas
(really, just me!)

"But even if we had splashed down waterfalls on hollowed logs and danced with bears in the moonlight, it wouldn't have been as great as my very most thankful thing."

"Mama, here you are with your soccer team. Was that your most thankful thing? You all won a trophy!"

Score:
5·4!!!

Regional CHAMP

"I had good friends on that team and I scored a goal once. But even if I had been the strongest, fastest player in the league, it wouldn't have been as wonderful as my most thankful thing."

"There you are playing your guitar on a stage. Were you nervous, Mama? Was that your most thankful thing?"

"I practiced a long time to be able to play that song, and I was proud to be in the concert. But even if I had become a famous rock star, it wouldn't have been as special as my very most thankful thing."

"I loved being the editor. But if I had become a real writer and written the best-selling book in the world and made a trillion dollars, it wouldn't top my most thankful thing."

"You looked really pretty at your prom, Mama. Was that your most thankful thing?"

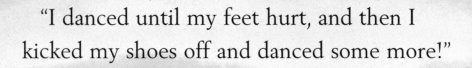
"I danced until my feet hurt, and then I kicked my shoes off and danced some more!"

Senior Prom !!!

Dance, Dance, Dance !!!

me and "hot" Scott!

"The prom was exciting, but even if it had been a royal ball, like in Cinderella, my most thankful thing would still be much, much better."

"It was a small part. But even if it had been the leading role in a big, important movie, and I had won an Academy Award, it wouldn't have topped my most thankful thing."

"I know, Mama! I know! You look so happy in this picture at your very first real job. Was that it?"

"My first job was super. But you know what?
Even if I got a job as President of the United States,
it wouldn't be as good as my most thankful thing."

"Oh, Mama, I figured it out. Here you are at your wedding with Daddy. You're smiling so big, Mama! That must be your most thankful thing."

"Marrying Daddy was truly a great thing. It could have been the best. But there's this one other thing…"

(first date)

ADMIT ONE
UNDER THE STARS AMPHITHEATER
JAMES TAYLOR
IN CONCERT

(my fortune at Kung Pao's Palace… second date!)

You will find the love of your life.

(I did!)

"Your most thankful thing must be awesome! It
must be amazing! I give up guessing. What is it, Mama?"

(15 minutes old!)

"Just when I thought I couldn't be any happier, I held you for the first time. I felt your soft, sweet breath on my skin and your warm, tiny body against mine.

 "And then I knew that nothing could ever be better, and that forevermore you would be my most thankful thing."

"Forevermore, Mama?"

"Forevermore."